Jake and Jen and the Sea of Sharks

Written by Chris Bradford

Illustrated by Korky Paul

Collins

Jake Jones, the legendary sailor, looked at the radar. "There is a giant storm ahead," he said.

Jen, the navigator on the boat, ordered, "Turn the wheel eight degrees west."

Jake steered them away from danger, but heavy waves capsized the boat.

Jake and Jen were thrown into the sea and battled for their lives.

A massive wave pushed Jake under.

"Catch this!" Jen shouted. She threw him a line. Jake grabbed the rope and she pulled him over.

"What a wild adventure!" Jake gasped as they clung to each other.

"This is worse than the jungle," agreed Jen.

The wind whipped around them and the sea raged, but at last the waves eased.

When the storm had passed, Jake and Jen looked for their boat.

"I can't spy it," said Jake.

Jen gazed at the empty skyline. "We're in the middle of the sea with no food or drink! How will we survive?"

They heard a splash.

Jake spun round. "What was that?"

Jen peered in fear at the sea. A school of fish swam by. "Just a dolphin, I think."

"Phew!" said Jake. "I was scared it was a …"

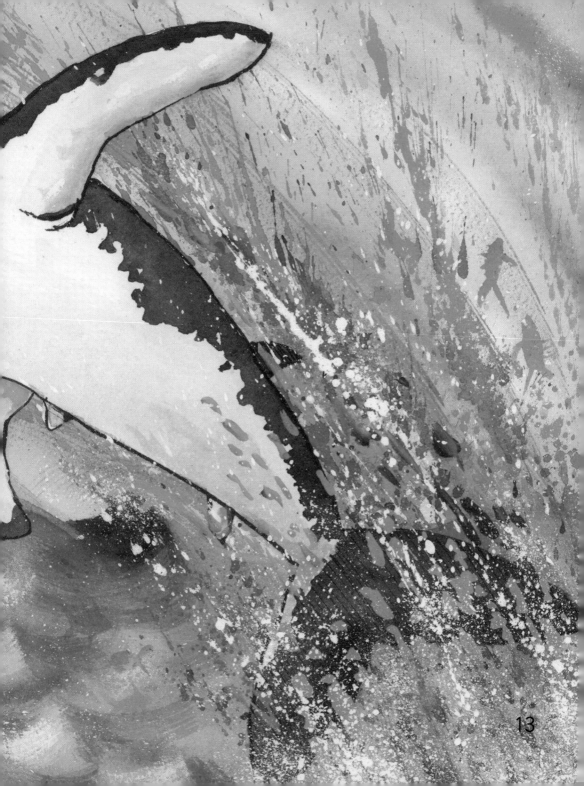

Jake and Jen dodged the shark as it lunged for them.

But the shark whirled round for another attack.
"What do we do now?" yelled Jake.

"Whack the shark on the nose to scare it away!"
Jen shouted.

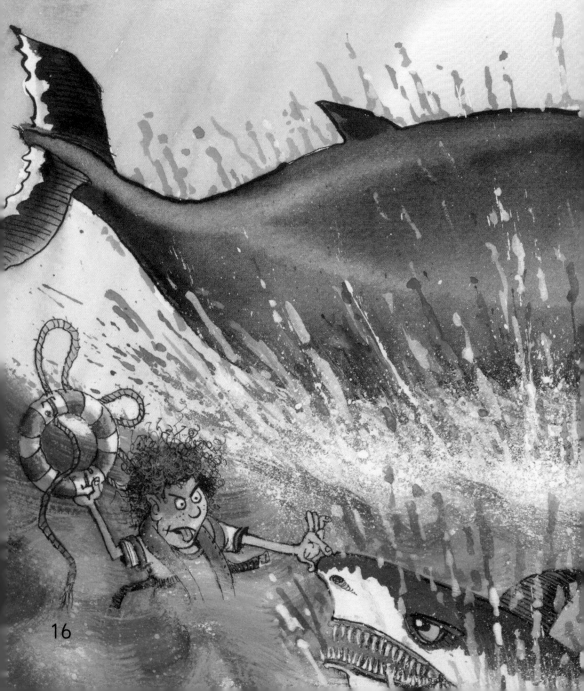

Jake held up the float to fend off the shark when a huge whale breached the waves.

The whale splashed down and sent the shark fleeing.

The giant wave then washed Jake and Jen on to dry land.

As they crawled out, their father belly flopped into the swimming pool again.

Jake and Jen giggled. "That will teach our brother to think we're shark bait!" said Jen.

After reading

Letters and Sounds: Phase 5

Word count: 298

Focus phonemes: /ai/ a, eigh /ee/ e, y /oo/ u /igh/ y /ch/ tch, t /c/ ch /j/ g, ge, dge /l/ le /f/ ph /w/ wh /v/ ve /s/ se /z/ se

Common exception words: of, to, the, into, said, do, our, their, were

Curriculum links: Science: Animals, including humans

National Curriculum learning objectives: Reading/word reading: read accurately by blending sounds in unfamiliar words containing GPCs that have been taught; Reading/comprehension: develop pleasure in reading, motivation to read, vocabulary and understanding by discussing word meanings, linking new meanings to those already known

Developing fluency

- Your child may enjoy hearing you read the book.
- Encourage your child to read the dialogue with expression, each of you taking the part of Jake or Jen.
- Challenge your child to reread their favourite pages from the book. Encourage them to read with expression, as if they are making a recording for the radio.

Phonic practice

- Challenge your child to find words in the book with these spellings and sounds:
  - /ee/ y (e.g. *empty*)
  - /igh/ y (e.g. *spy, sky(line)*)
- Ask your child to find words that contain /j/ g (e.g. *legendary, change*)

Extending vocabulary

- Look at pages 4 and 5. Ask your child to think of powerful words or phrases (synonyms) that could be used in place of the following:
  - **battled** (e.g. *struggled, grappled*)
  - **massive** (e.g. *monstrous, gigantic*)
  - **grabbed** (e.g. *clutched, snatched*)
- Turn to page 11 and discuss the phrase "school of fish". Explain that this is the official term for a group of fish.